Caleb's Colt

A Heartwarming Adventure of Hope and Change

Written by
JILL BRISCOE

Illustrated by Russ Flint

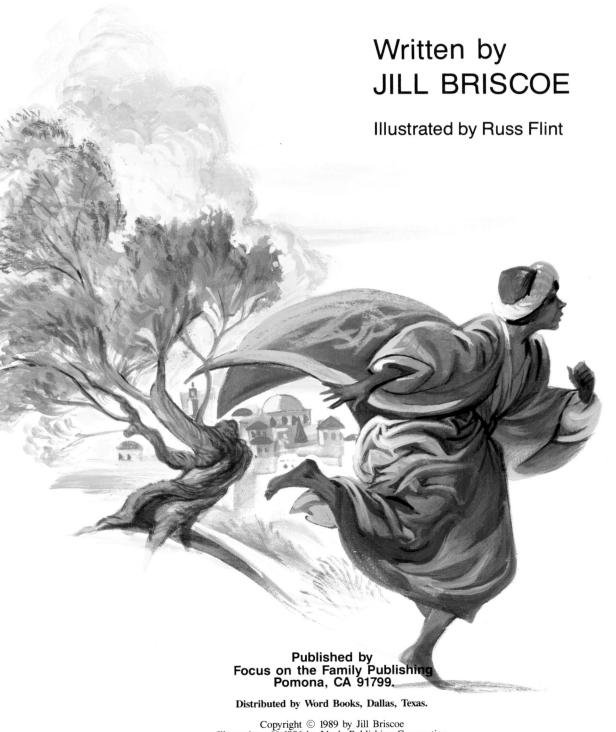

Published by
Focus on the Family Publishing
Pomona, CA 91799.

Distributed by Word Books, Dallas, Texas.

Designed by Julie Mammano

Library of Congress Catalog Card Number 89-11956
ISBN 0-929608-24-0

THE sun had just come up when Caleb raced into the courtyard, shouting, "Father! Father!"

"Over here," called his father.

"Will you go with me to tame my donkey?" asked Caleb.

His father looked at him with doubt and said, "That donkey's a stubborn one."

Caleb puffed and panted as he pulled on a rope around the neck of the donkey, Zimri. His father tried to shove the colt from behind.

Zimri watched them carefully. His eyes twinkled as if to say, "I love this game! Go on, try to move me. Let's play!"

"I'm beginning to wonder if we'll ever tame this colt," Caleb's father said, trying to tempt the animal to move by waving a juicy carrot under his nose.

"Oh, we will, we will," Caleb answered quickly, afraid that Zimri might be sold. He loved the little donkey with big, wide eyes and soft mouth.

"He's a hard one," replied Caleb's father. "We've never had such a nervous colt."

Caleb felt really worried now. "Let me try to ride him, Father, please. He knows me, and maybe he'll let me sit on him."

"Why not?" replied Caleb's father with an amused smile on his face.

The colt eyed Caleb and his father suspiciously. Then he stood still for a minute.

"Up you go, Caleb," shouted his father, and Caleb jumped onto the colt's back. Suddenly Zimri reared, throwing the boy right over the colt's head.

"Yeow!" Caleb yelled, landing upside down in a pile of leaves.

"This donkey's not ready to let anyone ride him, that's for sure," his father chuckled, helping Caleb to his feet.

As Caleb brushed the leaves off his tunic, he saw two of his father's friends, Peter and John, walking toward them. They had been helping Jesus, the teacher from Galilee. Caleb had heard about Jesus. He helped the sick get well. Many even said He raised people from the dead.

Peter and John greeted Caleb's father, and then Peter said, "Our Master, Jesus, needs to borrow your colt."

"Why?" Caleb said, as he tugged on the donkey's rope, trying to make him move.

"He needs a donkey to ride into Jerusalem tomorrow," John answered.

"Well, He doesn't need this one!" said Caleb. He rubbed a bump that had appeared on the side of his head.

"Oh, yes, He does," said John. "He sent us to bring this very colt."

"Don't worry," Peter added, smiling at the boy. "Jesus will know what to do with him!"

"Caleb," his father said, "help take the colt to Jesus."

Caleb was so excited, he felt his heart beat furiously. He was going to meet Jesus, the person who made blind men see and deaf men hear!

"Father, can Daniel come with me?" Caleb asked, quickly remembering his cousin and closest friend.

His father smiled. "If Daniel wants to go with you, he may."

Caleb untied the colt from the donkey stake. At first the colt refused to move.

"Come on, Zimri," Caleb said. "We're going to see Jesus."

The colt still wouldn't budge, so Caleb got behind him and pushed and pushed. When Caleb gave up, Zimri kicked his heels and brayed loudly. The colt showed his teeth in a naughty smile that seemed to say, "I'll come along with you, Caleb, but don't think I'm going to be good!"

Caleb led the colt to his house and called to his friend, "Daniel, come with me."

Daniel lived in the village of Emmaus, and when he wasn't in school, he helped his father and mother keep the inn in the village. As a special treat, he had been allowed to stay with Caleb for the holiday, the Feast of the Passover.

"Why, that's the stubbornest donkey I've ever seen," Daniel said, laughing.

"Jesus needs him," puffed Caleb as he pushed Zimri. "Though I can't imagine why. Come on, we have to take the colt to the Mount of Olives."

The two boys set off with the spirited colt. Once inside Jerusalem's city gates, the colt became terrified.

"Hang on, Caleb," Daniel shouted, trying to grab hold of the colt's rope.

"Get that donkey out of here!" a man with a cart shouted, pushing past them with his wares.

Then Zimri panicked. His nostrils flared, and he whinnied at the man, "Hee-haw! Hee-haw!"

"Watch the donkey!" one woman shouted to her children. "Keep away from his feet!"

In the center of the marketplace, the colt bumped into a baker carrying a basket of bread on his head. The loaves flew everywhere.

"What do you think you're doing?" shouted the man, shaking his fist at the boys. "Who's going to pay for my bread? Get that crazy donkey out of here!"

Such a loud voice was too much for the animal. He took off at a terrific pace, dragging Caleb and Daniel behind him.

By the time they arrived at the Mount of Olives, the boys were very glad to hand the colt over to someone else.

"There He is!" shouted Caleb. Jesus' smile was the kindest Caleb had ever seen. He looked like a king even though He wore the clothes of a poor man.

"Caleb and Daniel, bring the colt to Me," said Jesus. Zimri trotted right toward Jesus without being pushed or pulled.

"Thank you for letting Me use Zimri," Jesus said.

"Master," Caleb said with a gulp, wondering how Jesus knew their names, "Zimri won't let anyone ride him. Are you sure you want to use him?"

"Yes, Caleb. I know this stubborn colt." Jesus laughed and everyone around joined in. The boys felt their hearts smiling inside them at the sound of His laughter.

Taking the rough halter in His hand, Jesus looked with great kindness at the colt. The wide, brown eyes of the animal seemed to smile back as if to say, "I wouldn't do this for anyone else in the whole world."

Caleb and Daniel watched with amazement as Jesus mounted the donkey and set off down the hill toward Jerusalem. He rode along while men, women and children tore branches off the trees, waved them in the air and threw them on the ground in front of the colt's hooves.

Happy shouts filled the air. "The Son of God has come! The Savior is here! Jesus is the King! God bless the King of Israel!"

Daniel and Caleb couldn't believe their eyes. The colt behaved perfectly, picking his way over the palm branches and holding his head up proudly as if to say, "This is the most important day of my life!"

When they reached Jerusalem, Jesus
dismounted and turned the colt over to
Caleb and Daniel.

"Now you can ride him home," Jesus
said. "He won't throw you over his head
this time, Caleb."

Caleb took the animal from Jesus' hands,
wondering how He knew the colt had
thrown him before.

"I've never seen a colt ridden before he
was broken," Daniel said timidly to Jesus.

"He knows Me," Jesus replied. "I made
him." Then Jesus walked away, leaving
Caleb and Daniel gazing after Him.

"What did He mean?" Caleb asked
Daniel.

"I don't know," replied Daniel.

"Only God can make a donkey," sputtered
Caleb.

"I know," Daniel said very quietly.

As the two boys rode home, Daniel said, "Caleb, we're riding the colt, and he's being good! Jesus really did tame him."

"Wait till we tell Father and Mother about this," Caleb replied. "They won't believe us!"

Tumbling off the donkey, the boys rushed inside Caleb's house to tell their tale.

"Zimri let Jesus ride him," bubbled Caleb.

"And the colt didn't kick up his heels once," added Daniel.

"The people shouted, 'Jesus is the King,'" said Caleb.

"The Jewish and Roman leaders won't like that," his father replied. "Jesus will be in trouble."

A few days later, Daniel and Caleb heard some bad news from Simon, their friend who lived next door. "Jesus was arrested," he told them.

"Why?" the boys asked in astonishment.

"No one knows," said Simon.

"Perhaps we can find out," said Caleb, hoisting a batch of fresh bread onto his shoulder. "We're delivering bread to the governor's fortress."

"Then maybe you will," answered Simon, "since that's where the soldiers are guarding Jesus."

Inside the Roman fortress the boys found a servant girl who was happy to tell them all she knew. "I was sweeping the courtyard when the soldiers brought in Jesus. Two of His friends were with Him."

"Oh, that's good," sighed Caleb with relief. "That must have been Peter and John."

"Some friends they turned out to be," continued the girl. "One of them said he didn't know Him."

Caleb and Daniel looked at each other in horror.

"I don't blame him, mind you," continued the girl. "The governor, Pontius Pilate, had Jesus whipped. Perhaps His friends were afraid they would be whipped, too."

The two boys ran home to tell Caleb's father what had happened. The older man looked very upset when he heard the boys' report.

"If they have taken Jesus to the governor," he said, "they are likely to ask for the death sentence."

"But what has He done?" asked Caleb angrily.

"Some of the Jewish and Roman leaders hate Jesus because He's been saying He is God," replied Caleb's father.

"Only God can make donkeys," murmured Daniel.

"Father," asked Caleb, "do you think He is God?"

"Yes, my son, I do," replied Caleb's father quietly.

The boys slept lightly that night, tossing and turning in their beds. When they awoke, their first thoughts were about Jesus.

They wanted to go back to the governor's fortress, but Caleb's father sent them on errands. The boys ran down the colorful, narrow streets that wound in and out of the ancient stone buildings. Visitors filled the streets of Jerusalem for the Passover. When they started around one corner, a crowd blocked their way.

"Make way for the prisoners," shouted a soldier.

"Don't take Him," cried a woman.

"Look, He's fallen," gasped a man, standing in front of the boys.

A mob of angry men squashed the boys against a wall. They couldn't see anything and could only guess what was going on. They heard the crowd screaming, "Kill Him! Crucify Him!"

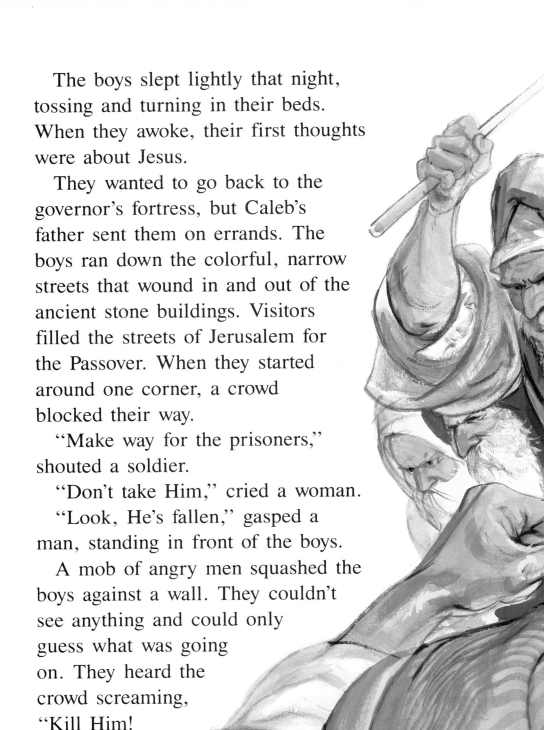

The boys took off running. They dashed to a nearby shop and asked the owner, "What's happening?"

"The Romans are taking three men to be crucified," the shopkeeper said. "One of them is that carpenter everyone is talking about, Jesus of Nazareth."

"We've got to stop them!" Caleb cried.

"And how are two boys like you going to do that?" inquired the shopkeeper. "Perhaps you intend to take on the armies of Rome all by yourselves?"

"But, but," sputtered Daniel, "He's God! They can't kill God!"

"Well now, if Jesus really is God, I don't think He will allow the soldiers to kill Him, do you?" asked the shopkeeper.

"I don't suppose so," muttered Caleb, but he felt confused and scared.

The boys raced for home through the streets, empty now of the busy sounds of buying and selling. When Caleb saw his father in front of their house, he shouted, "Father! They're going to kill Jesus!"

Caleb's father turned toward them, his face the saddest Caleb had ever seen it. "I know, my son. This is a terrible day."

It was noontime, and the sun was shining brightly. But all of a sudden, the sky turned dark as night.

"Even the sun hides its face from us," Daniel whispered.

Zimri, standing near the wall of the courtyard, swished his tail and tossed his head, his eyes wide and wild.

"The colt knows about Jesus," said Daniel. "Look at him!"

Suddenly, it was quiet—scary quiet. The birds weren't singing. The donkey stood perfectly still. Then the ground rolled and wobbled.

"It's an earthquake!" Caleb's father shouted. "God have mercy on us."

He took hold of the boys and threw his arms around them as they fell to the ground. As quickly as it had begun, the quaking ground ceased to rumble and roar. An unearthly stillness settled around them again.

The donkey was making little troubled noises, and Caleb ran to him, putting his arms around Zimri's warm neck to comfort him.

Suddenly, two friends of Caleb's father ran into the courtyard. "Jesus is dead," one said breathlessly. "They took Him outside the city with two other men. They nailed His hands and feet to a piece of wood, then hanged Him from this cross until He died!"

"Jesus dead?" exclaimed Caleb. "How could anyone kill Him?"

"He was so kind," said Daniel. "All He ever did was help people."

"What will happen now?" asked Caleb sadly.

"I don't know," replied his father with tears in his eyes.

Three days later, Caleb's father decided that his son should go away for a few days. Maybe he wouldn't feel so sad about the events of the past week.

"Caleb, how would you like to go home with Daniel to Emmaus?" he asked his son.

"Father, that would be wonderful!" replied Caleb.

Daniel smiled broadly. "We can play in the countryside."

The two boys packed their belongings and set off for the quiet village. Safely in Emmaus, Caleb and Daniel shared the events of the last few days with Daniel's parents.

"Who knows?" said his mother, shaking her head. "Many people believed Jesus was God and that He would redeem and set His people free. Look at all the miracles He did."

"He told us He made my colt," Caleb said.

"Only God can make a donkey," added Daniel.

All day the children helped Daniel's father clean and bake bread and prepare meat for the evening meal. Late that night, just as it was time to close, three strangers knocked on the inn door.

"It's late," grumbled Daniel's father. "I was just about to bolt the door for the night. Who are these people who come at this hour, expecting food and lodging?"

"It's dark," Daniel's mother reminded him. "We must take them in. It's too late for them to go on to the next village. There are robbers about, and the roads are dangerous."

"Yes, you're right," replied Daniel's father. "Daniel! Caleb! Come quickly! Set the table. Make sure the guests are comfortable."

When Daniel and Caleb ran into the inn, they found three guests sitting at the table, talking earnestly.

Suddenly, they heard a braying in the courtyard.

"Go outside, Caleb," Daniel said, "and take care of the man's donkey. It will need hay and water."

Caleb dashed outside and right into his own colt! "What are you doing here?" he asked Zimri with astonishment.

Whirling around, Caleb raced back into the kitchen. "Aunt! Uncle!" he called. "My colt, the one Jesus rode into Jerusalem, is here!"

"Well, what of it?" asked Daniel's father. "The colt was probably hired from your father for one of the visitors to Jerusalem."

"My father told me he would never hire out that colt—not after Jesus rode him into Jerusalem that day."

Daniel's father stared at Caleb. "Maybe your father changed his mind," he said.

Before Caleb could reply, Daniel rushed into the kitchen. "He's—He's gone!" he stammered.

"Who's gone?" asked his father.

"The man, one of the three men who was just here! I saw His hands when He tore the loaf of bread apart," said Daniel, his voice wavering. "They—they had holes in the palms."

"Jesus!" shouted Caleb.

"Yes! Jesus!" answered Daniel, his face shining with wonder. "Where did He go?"

"The door was locked! I bolted it myself," said Daniel's father. "No one can leave unless they have the key."

"The God who made donkeys has no trouble with locked doors," Daniel said with a laugh.

The family hurried into the dining room. The two men stood with their arms around each other, crying with joy.

"Our hearts were so happy when He talked with us," said one.

"We should have known it was Jesus," said the other.

"When He took the bread in His hands, I saw the nail prints in them. That's when I recognized Him," said the first.

"God has visited us," said Daniel's father in awe.

"He really is God's Son. He was dead, but now He's alive!" said the other man. "He came to give us new life."

Caleb left the men and ran outside to feed and water his colt. The animal had the loveliest light in his eyes. He looked so content, as if someone had given him a loving pat on his head and stroked his rough mane. He looked for all the world as if he were smiling.

"Jesus was here," said Caleb happily to Zimri.

The colt brayed as if to say, "Yes, Jesus was here, Caleb. He told me He won't be needing me anymore. He's going home!"